A Friend for Carlita

written by Lynette Dyer Vuong

illustrated by Joe Boddy

To my mother
who loved telling others that Jesus loves them

Library of Congress Catalog Card Number 88-63566
© 1989, The STANDARD PUBLISHING Company, Cincinnati, Ohio
Division of STANDEX INTERNATIONAL Corporation. Printed in U.S.A.

Something red caught Kathy's eye as she and her friends made a snowman at recess. She glanced over at the monkey bars, and saw that the red thing was a hat the new girl was wearing.

The new girl, Carlita, sat in the same position she had been in since the class first came out for recess. Her head hung down. Her long braids drooped in her lap as she kicked at the snow.

Kathy patted snow onto the snowman, then turned to her friends, Jean and Linda. "Why don't we ask Carlita to play with us?" she said. "She's new and doesn't have any friends."

Linda made a face. "She probably doesn't know how to make a snowman. They don't have snow in El Salvador where she used to live."

Jean nodded. "It's more fun with just the three of us. The bell will be ringing in a minute anyhow."

Kathy shrugged and bent over to get a handful of snow.

"Don't forget tonight's Girls' Club meeting," Linda reminded them. "Have you got your stuff ready for the Christmas package we're sending to our missionary in El Salvador?"

The school bell rang just then and the three girls started back to the building.

"We should invite Carlita to our club meeting tonight," Kathy said. "Remember what our leader, Mrs. Jenkins, said about . . ."

"Yeah, but she didn't mean Carlita," Linda said, frowning. "She's different and probably wouldn't like our club anyway."

Back in the classroom, the girls took their seats. Kathy opened her math book, but her mind was still on what Mrs. Jenkins had said about their missionary in El Salvador. She was thinking too about the Christmas package their club was sending to the children at the school where the missionary taught.

"We can all be missionaries," Mrs. Jenkins had told them. "A missionary is anyone who helps others to know how much Jesus loves them. We can all do that, can't we?"

"Yes, we can," Kathy said to herself as she silently prayed, "Jesus, help me show Carlita that You love her and that I love her too."

The closing bell signaled the end of the school day. Carlita pulled on her hat with the red pom-poms and started for the door. Kathy hurried after her.

"Which way do you go home?" she asked Carlita.

"Down Oh-lee-vare Street," Carlita said, pointing.

Kathy could tell that Carlita was trying to say Oliver Street.

"I live on Oliver Street too," she told Carlita. "Let's walk home together."

Carlita's eyes sparkled. "Oh, yes, I like that!"

As they walked along, Kathy told Carlita about their Girls' Club and the Christmas project they were planning. Then she asked, "How would you like to come to our meeting tonight, Carlita? We could go together."

"I like that! I'll ask Mama if I can go. Can you come with me?" Carlita answered.

Carlita's mother met them at the door. Her eyes brightened as Carlita told her about the Girls' Club and their Christmas project.

Then Carlita led Kathy over to a table where a manger scene lay. In the scene, Mary was sitting by the manger and Joseph standing nearby. A shepherd leaned on a crook, while two others knelt. A donkey gazed into the manger, and the sheep seemed about to bleat their praises to the newborn child.

Kathy reached for the baby Jesus. "It's precious! I love it!" she said.

"Papa made it," Carlita said, smiling again.

Then she picked up a block of wood with only a head carved at the top. She handed it to Kathy.

"Here is a wise man," she said. "Tonight maybe it's finished."

"I wish the others could see these too!" Kathy exclaimed.

Carlita only smiled, then said, "You come for me at six-thirty, yes?"

That evening as they came into the church, all the girls were carrying paper bags. Carlita had a bag too. She had brought several bars of soap for the Christmas package.

"Does anybody have any ideas for our Christmas party?" Mrs. Jenkins asked as they worked.

Kathy glanced at Carlita and then down at the gifts they were packing. "How about an El Salvador party?" she said. "It would be another way of sharing Christmas with the ones we're sending the package to."

"That's a lovely idea," said Mrs. Jenkins. "And maybe you'd like to take pictures at the party too. We could send them to the boys and girls in El Salvador, like they did last year after they got our package."

"That'd be neat," Linda said, smiling. "Can you help us make a piñata, Mrs. Jenkins?"

Carlita's face lit up. "I can help. I always help Papa make the piñata. Every Christmas."

"You should see the manger scene her dad made," Kathy told them. "Oh, Carlita! Do you suppose he'd let us borrow it for the party?"

Carlita didn't say anything. She just opened her bag.

The girls gasped as she pulled out a tiny sheep and the manger with baby Jesus in it. Then she placed them gently on a table.

Jean reached over and picked up the little lamb.

"It's beautiful," she whispered. "I never imagined . . ."

"I hope you'll come to our club every week," Linda said. "We always have a good time. And we learn about Jesus. He's our best friend."

"Our best friend?" Carlita said. Her eyes glowed as she glanced from one girl to another. "I'm glad you told me that. Since I came here I have no friends. But now I have all of you and Jesus too. This is the best Christmas in the whole world!"